THE
ACCOMPANIST

BOOKS BY NINA BERBEROVA

The Accompanist   1988

The Italics Are Mine   1969

Nina Berberova

———⊰⊱———

THE
ACCOMPANIST

Translated from the Russian by
Marian Schwartz

ATHENEUM

New York   1988

Atheneum
Macmillan Publishing Company
866 Third Avenue, New York, N.Y. 10022

ISBN 0-689-11989-5

10 9 8 7 6 5 4 3 2 1

First American Edition

Printed in the United States of America

THE
ACCOMPANIST

THESE NOTES were acquired for me by a Mr L.R., who bought them from a junk dealer on the rue Roquette, along with an engraving depicting the town of Pskov in the year 1775 and a lamp, a brass lamp, which had once burned paraffin but had been quite soundly wired for electricity. In the course of buying the engraving, Mr L.R. asked the junk man whether he had anything else Russian. 'I do,' replied the dealer, and from a dusty cupboard standing in the corner of his old shop he took a *quadrillé* notebook, the kind that has served certain people, but primarily the young, for writing diaries.

The junk dealer elaborated that he had purchased the notebook along with some sheet music and two or three Russian books (which he could not find, unfortunately) about five years before for fifty centimes in a cheap hotel where a Russian woman had lived and died. The landlady sold off (in payment for the room) her dresses and linen and other things – all that is left after a woman vanishes.

L.R. first listened to all this, and only then did he

open the notebook. The first lines he fell on caught his interest, so he paid his money and took the lamp in one hand and in the other the engraving, pressing the notebook under his arm. Once home he read the whole thing *without ever working out* who had written it.

I have altered one or two things in these notes because not everyone will prove equally ill-informed. She who wrote and did not burn this notebook lived among us, and many people knew, saw, and heard her. Death, as is evident, caught her off guard. If it was illness, then it was a brief and intense illness that prevented her from putting her earthly affairs in order; if it was suicide, then it was so impulsive that it did not leave the deceased time to settle any scores.

In any event, she left behind this notebook, as a passenger leaves behind a parcel when he hops from a train in motion.

ONE

———————⊰•⊱———————

TODAY IT is one year since mama died. Several times
I've tried to say that word out loud, but my lips have
lost the habit of it. It was odd and nice. Then it passed.
Some people call their stepmothers 'mama', others call
their husband's mother that; once I heard an elderly
gentleman call his wife 'mama' (she was about ten
years younger than he). I had one mama, and there
will never be another. Her name was Ekaterina
Vasilievna Antonovskaya. She was thirty-seven when
I was born, and I was her first and only child.

She was a music teacher, and none of her students
knew that she gave birth to me. They knew only that
she was seriously ill for an entire year and went away
somewhere. They waited patiently for her return.
Before my birth some of them had come to her at home.
When I appeared, mama stopped having them come.
She was out for entire days at a time. The old cook took
care of me. It was a small apartment, two rooms. The
cook slept in the kitchen, mama and I in the bedroom,
and the other room was taken up by the piano, so we

called it the piano room. That was where we ate. On New Year's Day the boy students sent mama flowers; the girl students gave her portraits of Beethoven and death masks of Liszt and Chopin. Once, on a Sunday, we were walking down the street – I was nine years old – and we ran into the two Sveshnikova sisters, who were just then finishing high school. They took to kissing and squeezing mama so that I started screaming from fright.

'Who is this, dear Katish Vasilievna?' the young ladies asked.

'This is my daughter,' mama replied.

From that day the word was out, and in one week mama lost three lessons. A month later she was left with just Mitenka.

It didn't matter to Mitenka's parents whether or not mama was married or how many children she had or by whom exactly. Mitenka was a talented boy and they paid well, but one couldn't live off Mitenka alone. We let the cook go, sold the piano, and without losing any time, moved to Petersburg. There we picked up some Conservatory contacts. Mama was loved there as well. Slowly, laboriously, she carved out a life for herself and for me. And by the first winter she was again running all day long, in the wet, in the frost. Me, she enrolled in the Conservatory in the preparatory class. By then I already played quite competently.

It never occurred to me to give much thought to what mama went through when she abandoned our home town, where she had once grown up – alone with her mother, also a music teacher. Her father, my grandfather, died early on, and it was just the two of them, like we were now, and everything was very similar, only there was no *shame*. Grandmother sent mama to Petersburg at age sixteen to study. She graduated from the Conservatory, returned to N., gave a concert, played at charity evenings, and little by little started working with young beginners.

I never thought about her living alone, after her own mother's death, how it must have been for her to turn thirty, or what happened after, or who my father was. The drawers of her desk didn't lock, but I never ran across any photographs or letters. I remember once, I was very young at the time, I asked her if I had a papa. She said:

'No, my Sonechka, we don't have a papa. Our papa died.'

That's just what she said: 'our', and we had a good cry together.

I found out the whole story very simply. I was fifteen when mama's friend, a French teacher at the N. high school, came to Petersburg. It was early evening, about six o'clock. Mama wasn't home. I was stretched out on our narrow old sofa reading Tolstoy. The doorbell. Kisses. Exclamations. 'My, how you've grown! What a big girl you are now!'

She and I sat together for quite a while. It was evening and the lamp was lit; someone was singing on the other side of the wall. We talked, reminiscing about years long past in N., about my childhood. I don't know how it happened that she told me about my father being a former student of mama's and all of nineteen at the time. Before him she had never loved anyone. Later he married and had children. I didn't ask his first name or his last.

Mama came home. She was over fifty now. She was rather grey and little – like most mamas actually – and freckles had started appearing on her hands. I myself couldn't have said what was going on inside me: I was sorry for her, so sorry that I felt like lying down and crying and not getting up until I'd cried my heart out. The thought of her shame drove me wild; had he come in right then I would have hurled myself at him, punched him in the eye, bit him in the face. But even more than that I was ashamed. I realized that my mama was my disgrace, just as I was hers. And our whole life was one irreparable shame.

But that passed. At the Conservatory no one ever asked me about my father – not that I ever got that close to anyone. It was wartime. I had become an adult. Gradually I had grown used to the idea that I would have to choose a career for myself – I already had a craft.

I called my father 'the offender'. Later I realized that that wasn't quite right. He was nineteen years old. For him my mother had been nothing but a step on the path to maturity. More than likely he never even suspected that she, at her age, was a virgin. And she? How passionately and hopelessly, notwithstanding their closeness, she must have loved in order to enter into a liaison with a man young enough to be her son and to give birth from that – a brief and for her unique liaison – to a daughter. What remained from all that in her memory and in her heart?

And now – revolution. For each person the old life ended at a different moment. For one, when he boarded the boat at Sevastopol. For another, when Budenny's Red Guards entered his steppe village. For me – in the peaceful life of Petersburg. There were no classes at the Conservatory. Mitenka, who had already been hanging around Petersburg for a month (he had come to study composition) came to see us on October 25th, in the morning. Mama had caught a cold. Mitenka played, then we had lunch, then Mitenka dozed. Oh, how I remember that day! For some reason I was very busy sewing something. In the evening the three of us played cards. I even remember that we had beef and cabbage for dinner.

Mitenka was the son of wealthy merchants in N. He was mama's old student from the time of shame, so to speak. He was a phlegmatic young man, about three years my senior, utterly indifferent to life in general and to his own person in particular. He had peculiarities; he was a scatterbrained sleepyhead whom tutors had a hard time teaching cleanliness. He was not so much devoted to music as he was a sort of conduit for certain chaotic sounds which through him burst out of nonexistence into reality. When he entered the composition class he shocked everyone by being avant-garde and revolutionary. But in conversation he was helpless and could neither make a point nor defend his views. Mama became more and more discouraged over his cacophonies, which were turning into a crude and terrible obsession.

I didn't care about him one way or the other. That autumn, after so many years away from N., I was really seeing him for the first time. He was twenty. He was not handsome. He had started to shave but didn't always, and the hair on his head was already thinning. In addition, he wore a big silver-rimmed pince-nez, had a nasal twang, and breathed heavily through his nose while he listened. But he loved mama very much. He apologized for his 'chorales' based on words by Khlebnikov and said that the time would come when there would be nothing: no roads, no bridges, no sewers – just music.

My Conservatory friends who visited us considered Mitenka a cretin, but no one questioned his musical genius. I had no use for his chorales or his affection. I was concerned with events, I was concerned with the future, I was especially concerned with a certain Evgenii Ivanovich, lately departed for Moscow, who had worked in the Conservatory office and with whom I had had the following conversation a month before:

He: 'Are you a good guesser?'

I: 'I think so.'

'There's something I want to tell you but I can't. You have to guess.'

'Okay.'

'Now you answer: yes or no?'

My heart started thumping.

'Yes . . .'

But it was not Evgenii Ivanovich who was to give my life a new turn but foolish, pale-faced Mitenka: Evgenii Ivanovich went to Moscow and never came back. He did not vindicate my matrimonial hopes. That winter, when I thought over our conversation and still had hopes that he would write, that he would come, sometimes I started wondering whether he might not have been declaring his love at all, whether he might have had something completely different in mind: for example, he might have wanted to ask me to lend him a small sum, or to say hello to someone for him, maybe someone he cared for. Oh, let it be! Let us turn instead to a new introduction that had 'fateful' consequences for me. In the winter of 1919 Mitenka introduced me to Maria Nikolaevna Travina.

TWO

————— ✥◦✥ —————

I was eighteen years old. I had graduated from the Conservatory. I was neither smart nor pretty; I had no expensive dresses and no outstanding talent. In short, I didn't have much going for me. The famine was beginning. My mama's dream of me giving music lessons was not to be – there were barely enough lessons for her. Once in a while an odd job would come along for me at musical evenings, in factories or workers' clubs. I remember a few times – in return for soap and lard – I went somewhere in the dockyards and played dance tunes all night long. Then I got a regular job, on Saturdays – for bread and sugar – in the Railroad Club at the Nikolaevsky Railway. First I played the Internationale, then Bach, then Rimsky-Korsakov, then Beethoven, then Mitenka's 'chorales' (which were then coming into vogue). But I couldn't support myself on one Saturday job. So I found an opera singer who needed an accompanist, which took up three hours a day; it was a long way away, and there were no trams. And until he got me through the various official registries for a ration card more than two months passed. But at last that too was arranged.

The singer had been a rather well-known baritone. Now he was coming up on seventy, he smelled of cheap tobacco and the wine cellar, and his hands were black from working in the kitchen and chopping wood. He was getting so thin that each month his clothes hung more and more loosely. Buttons came off; elbows and knees wore through. He never washed, only shaved his chin and upper lip on rare occasions, and then powdered himself so heavily that it sprinkled off. And it seemed to me like plaster flaking off him, like off an old crumbling wall, and that he smelled not of the wine cellar but simply of damp earth.

'Sonechka,' he used to say to me, 'why is it you're so skinny? You won't get anywhere on your youth alone. You need curves, curves! You have a paw like a chicken's, a leg like a goat's, and a bosom like a cat's. Ah, what will ever become of you, my child, with a figure like that!'

He was sincerely distressed over my future. I was happy to have learned his repertoire and be bringing home what rations I did. That winter he caught a chill and was laid up. Everything in his apartment quickly fell to pieces: the pipes froze, it was two degrees in his rooms, the piano strings broke, the paraffin ran out. A doctor was sent from the Union. I continued to come every day. Some friends showed up, some ladies. There was semolina. I was sent to the neighbours for salt; I ran to the distribution centre for jam. Then it was all over: he died on his dirty sheets, on his torn pillowcase, and there was a lot of fuss over his funeral. Taking care of the dead man was draining.

I was out of a job. My boots were made from a rug, my dress from a tablecloth, my winter coat from mama's cloak, my hat from some gold-embroidered sofa cushions. I might live, but I also might not – and somehow it didn't much matter which. Mama would look at me with curiosity and sadness. Mitenka wheezed through his nose and sat up late with us, watching me darn, drink tea, play, or, ignoring him, read. One evening he came over, looking very preoccupied; Maria Nikolaevna Travina needed an accompanist, permanent, not temporary, perhaps to go abroad.

Mitenka was preoccupied because, first of all, he was trying to convey to me the conditions of the job in a businesslike, coherent way, and that, like everything practical, was tough for him. Secondly, he felt sorry for me, sorry that I was going to leave mama and him. He did not like things to change.

At first mama was upset. Maybe it would be better if I did become an accompanist, not a music teacher, if I broke away from her to lead my own life? I looked at her. This was an old woman already, who in recent years had become stooped and shrunken, whose eyes were lifeless and hair grey, who sometimes couldn't summon up the right words. She couldn't be an adviser for me, a support. I tried to look at myself objectively. There was no way I could help her. At one time I had been a hindrance to her in life, and now I was no consolation. Something dimly told me that I would never bring her happiness. Did she love me? Yes, she did. But there was a pathetic gap in that love, and when she kissed me I always felt as if she were trying to smooth over that gap – for her sake, for mine, for Mitenka's, for God knows who else's.

I didn't say anything. Mitenka sat with his arms stretched across the table and elaborated. I was being offered a position, a permanent position with a salary, with board; I would be taken to Moscow, to the provinces, I would be my own person.

'As a lady's maid? A lady's companion?' I asked suddenly out of angry curiosity.

Mitenka even laughed, and mama smiled as well. We should have been very happy, but we weren't. But clocks tick too without happiness, and rain falls without happiness, but life goes on nonetheless. How beautiful God's world is, and how rightly everything in it is ordered!

So I put on my rug boots and all my masquerade-type clothes typical of the time, which made me look as if I were a moulting, faded youth from some nomadic Asiatic tribe, and set off to see Maria Nikolaevna Travina.

Petersburg. 1919. Snowdrifts. Silence. Cold and hunger. A belly swollen from millet. Feet unwashed for a month. Windows chinked with rags. Greasy stove soot. I walk into the building. A large building on Furshtatskaya Street. A lift suspended between floors.

In it – excrement frozen solid. A door on the third floor. I knock. No answer. I ring the bell. To my surprise, it works. A maid wearing a cap and proper shoes opens the door. It's warm. My God, it's warm! No, this is not to be believed: a huge tile stove so hot you can't get near it. Rugs. Curtains. Fresh flowers – pale blue hyacinths – in a basket on an end table. A box of expensive cigarettes. A blue – almost like the hyacinths – smoky cat arches his back when he sees me, and a woman, for some reason in a white dress – or a housedress (I can't tell the difference), or maybe it's what you put on under a dress – sees me and walks towards me, smiling, holding out a hand with long pink fingernails. Her stockings are pink as well. Pink stockings!

She is ten years older than I and of course does not hide the fact, because she is beautiful and I am not. She is tall and has a relaxed, strong, healthy body. I'm small, tense, sickly looking, although I'm never ill. She has smooth black hair tied in a knot at her nape; my hair is fair and lifeless, and I cut it short and try to curl it. She has a beautiful round face, a big mouth, a smile of ineffable charm, and green-streaked black eyes; my eyes are pale, my face triangular and high-cheekboned, my teeth narrow and widely spaced. She walks, talks, sings so confidently, her hands accompany her words and movements so calmly and evenly, and in her lurks a burning, a spark – divine or demonic – a distinct 'yes' and 'no'. Around me (this I sense) there sometimes forms a hazy cloud of hes-

itancy, indifference, boredom, in which I tremble the
way nocturnal insects tremble in sunlight before
they're blinded and die. And when we walked out – she
ahead, without any affectation, without tension,
bowing, smiling, radiating beauty and health, and I
behind, always in a slightly crushed dress, as if a little
dried out, also bending, bowing, and trying to hold my
hands like this and not that – when we both walked
out: *Well, what more do you want?* I would say to
myself. *What more do you want out of life? To get
even? How? And with whom? Behave yourself stiller
than the water, lower than the grass. You're not going
to be acknowledged in this life – and there isn't a next!*

She sat me down in an armchair, took my hands in
hers, unbuttoned my collar herself so that I wouldn't
be too hot. Then she told me to take off my coat and
called the maid in and asked her to serve tea. She
looked at me with inexpressible attention; there was
concern in her eyes, concern and curiosity. At first she
only asked me questions: how old am I, what am I like,
what do I like, am I willing to go away with her if
necessary? Later, when tea was brought in, she poured
for herself and for me, put thin slices of buttered white
bread covered with ham and cheese on my plate, and
started talking herself, turning aside slightly so as not
to embarrass me. And I ate and ate and ate.

'I've known your mama's name for a long time,
Sonechka,' she said. 'I'll call you Sonechka because
you're still such a young girl, and that, if I can be
frank, is perhaps the one thing in you that scares me.

No, it doesn't scare me, but it does worry me a little. Won't you be bored with me? Won't you get homesick for Petersburg? After all, we might go far away, very far away . . . You probably can't even imagine how far. I rehearse a lot, four hours a day without fail, no matter what, making no allowances for myself, and that means for you as well. Then there are the concerts. After all, this is going to be a real tour, Sonechka, my first real tour, and it must be a success.'

I made a movement.

'I'm known only in Petersburg,' she continued, having taken note of it. 'I want more. I'm very ambitious. Talent doesn't come without ambition. You have to be ambitious, Sonechka, and I'm going to teach you that.'

I shuddered, but this time she didn't notice anything.

She talked. I listened. I realized that life might tie us together for many years to come, that this conversation would not be repeated. That's the way it is: the more accustomed people get to one another, the less likely they are to feel a need to talk about themselves. This conversation might turn out to be the only one of its kind. I sensed that, but still I kept nodding off, and I knew that I would fall asleep at any moment.

I tried to tell myself that I ought to be catching every word, that all this would stand me in good stead sometime in the future. Between us a lamp under a low silk shade had been lit; the curtains on the windows shut out the white twilight, her low gentle voice washed over me, her perfume scented the air, and my lips could still feel the recent touch of the delicate, cool ham fat. My legs were getting heavier and heavier. I set them like posts in front of me and sort of forgot about them, swimming in a sweet drowsiness where shadows rose to meet my tired eyes, took me in their arms, and slowly rocked my head, while at the same time I was making a superhuman effort to keep my eyes – drunk from warmth and satiety – open.

Now she was talking about her years of study, about her marriage, about her performances in the provinces during the war, about the fact that life, her whole life, still lay ahead of her. 'And of you, Sonechka,' she added. About countries overseas where maybe, 'just maybe', we would go one day, about Moscow, about Nezhdanova, about the romances Mitenka had dedicated to her, and about much much more, until she saw that I was looking at her with heavy, inert eyes.

'I've completely talked your head off, my dear friend!' she exclaimed. 'Forgive me.'

I stood up. She gave me some music, told me to come back in two days, and walked me to the door. And there she embraced me, kissing me on both cheeks.

THREE

———————◆◈◆———————

WALKING OUT of Maria Nikolaevna's I saw that it was late evening; there was darkness and snow was falling. The wind icing up my wet face immediately wiped away my sleep. What I had just seen I had seen for the first time, and the words I had just heard were to me utterly new. What was there about them? Nothing special. The main thing was that although I couldn't remember them and barely understood them, the way I had been spoken to and exactly who had been speaking was so extraordinary. Never in my life had I met a woman like that. From her emanated some mysterious, magnificent, and vanquishing equilibrium.

But when I thought about the hyacinths, about the maid, about the warmth and cleanliness, something inside me rebelled and I asked myself: does all this really in fact exist, and won't someone exact retribution for it? After all, if it were to happen to mama and me, to my baritone, to the thousands of others whose fingers were freezing off, whose teeth were crumbling, whose hair was falling out from malnutrition, cold, fear, filth, wouldn't retribution be exacted, comrade Chekists, for that apartment, that woman, that smoky cat? Wouldn't someone ensconce in that living room some metalworker's lice-ridden family, who would use the grand piano for a toilet and force her to clean it out every morning – with her pink hands? Isn't that what you call 'civic duty'? Was all that really going to be left intact? And were all of us – stripped, robbed, hungry, broken – going to stand for it? The Dutch cheese, and the stout log with the brown bark in the stove, and the milk in the saucer in which the kitty licked her tongue?

These thoughts made me hot in the chest. Tears and snow froze on my nose and cheeks. I wiped them away with my cuff and ran on, noiselessly in my rug boots, clutching the music under my arm. And through this hatred and bitterness, which had come over me for the first time in my life with such force and in which I felt I was breathing easier than I had in my sickly sweet and feeble indifference to everything, I suddenly remembered Maria Nikolaevna Travina herself, who kissed me on both cheeks and looked at me so attentively and tenderly. And at that moment she seemed to me such a wild, inaccessible perfection that I cried even harder, sobbed, and kept on running, running down the street, not knowing myself why I was running or where, or what our home, our room, mama had to do with me, or what on earth I was, or this city: Who needed it? And what was life? And God? Where was He? Why didn't He make us all exactly like He did her?

The next day I sat down to the piano first thing. The scores were quite varied: there were opera arias, there were love songs by Glinka, and modern music, and some unusual vocalizations that I had never heard before. I worked all day and the following morning. At three o'clock I was at Furshtatskaya. The piano was a magnificent concert Blüthner. Maria Nikolaevna vocalized for an hour, and then I had tea and pastry and at her request played her some Schubert. She listened and thanked me. In that time the phone rang two times in the next room. Someone answered it but did not call for her. Then she sang, and sang . . .

I know there are people who don't acknowledge singing: someone strikes a pose, opens his mouth (either naturally, and then it's ugly, or else affectedly, and then it's ridiculous), trying to maintain an expression of ease, inspiration, and wisdom, exaggeratedly shouts (or bellows) some not-always-successfully-strung-together words, sometimes senselessly hurried, sometimes chopped up, like for charades, sometimes awkwardly repeated several times.

But when she took a breath (not theatrically but just as simply as we take a breath of mountain air when we stick our head out of a train window) and spread her large, beautiful lips and a pure, strong, full-to-the-brim sound suddenly rang out above me, I suddenly realized that this was something immortal and indisputable, something which makes the heart contract and gives reality to the human being's dream of having wings and suddenly becoming weightless. A tearful joy suddenly overtook me. My fingers shook, getting lost in the black keys; I counted to myself, afraid of disappointing her at the very outset in my effort, but I felt a shudder pass down my spinal column. This was a dramatic soprano with magnificent, resilient high notes and deep clear low notes.

'One more time, Sonechka,' she said, and we repeated the aria. I don't remember what it was. I think it was Elizabeth's aria from *Tannhäuser*.

Then she rested for five minutes, petted the cat, drank half a cup of cold tea, and had me tell her about N., about my childhood. But I had nothing to tell her. She couldn't want to hear about Mitenka, could she? No. Anything but Mitenka. Thank God, she knew him well, after all, her husband was Mitenka's mother's first cousin. Yes, certainly he was talented, but there were times when he couldn't remember his own name.

Once again she sang, and I, still tentatively, still timidly, but conscientiously, accompanied her in this marvel, which felt like flying, or soaring, and there were moments when again a needle entered my heart and pierced it through. Several times she interrupted me, gave instructions, and asked me to start again from the beginning. She kept looking at me, listening to me. Was she satisfied with me?

At half past six a loud bell rang.

'Wait a moment,' Maria Nikolaevna said. 'That's for me.'

She went out into the foyer and I heard her open the door.

'I called twice,' said a loud male voice, 'but they told me you were busy and couldn't come to the telephone. What's the matter? Is it really that hard for you to come to the phone?'

'Hush, Senya, hush,' she replied. 'I have my lesson, a rehearsal. The accompanist is here.'

'To hell with them all! I called to take you for a ride. The car is downstairs. I wanted to go at four, and I was held up. I wanted to go at five, and there was no driver. I only just now got away.'

'It's almost seven now. Where could we go? Pavel Fyodorovich will be home any minute.'

The man evidently wanted to say something in reply, but I got the feeling she had covered his mouth with her hand. They were whispering out there. Then everything got quiet. Maria Nikolaevna came back into the living room.

And indeed, not a quarter of an hour passed before Pavel Fyodorovich came home.

'My husband,' said Maria Nikolaevna, rising to greet him, 'Sonechka Antonovskaya.' And we shook hands.

I scarcely had time to think that here I was meeting a man and I already had a secret from him, already I was a conspirator against him, when Maria Nikolaevna, walking away towards the window, said:

'Senya just drove by. He called to take me for a ride. What insolence – and all because I hadn't come to the telephone when he called.'

'So why didn't you go? It's snowing outside, it's marvellous, honest-to-goodness powder!'

She did not reply. I stood looking at the floor. Pavel Fyodorovich sat down on the nearest chair. He was wearing military boots. I raised my head. He had on a service jacket and he had a beard. His hair was longer than was usual but not 'artistic'. I'd say it was more 'merchantish'. His appearance was as ordinary as could be, if on the modest side. He looked about forty-five.

We ate as a threesome. I tried not to eat too greedily, but still, by the end of dinner, unaccustomed as I was to eating like that, I was so weighted down that I had a hard time controlling myself. The maid passed the serving dishes, first to Maria Nikolaevna, then to me, then to Pavel Fyodorovich. In the big dining room I was even more ill at ease than in the living room, to which I had managed to get somewhat accustomed. The conversation was almost exclusively about me. Having drunk a glass of red wine, I must have got a little tipsy; in the sideboard mirror on which my glance fell from time to time I saw that I'd become all red and puffy. *'She told him that* he *had come because she's not sure of me yet.'* And I let out an out-of-place laugh. *I have to earn her trust.*

What for? To betray it later? I dropped my spoon in my dish, and my compote splashed on the tablecloth. *I have to earn it, deserve it, so that later, when the time comes, out of the blue, I can shield her from some misfortune, rescue her suddenly, serve her so slavishly that she doesn't even know it's me. I have to make myself indispensable, irreplaceable, utterly faithful, without a thought for myself . . . Or else some day betray her, all her beauty and her voice, just to prove that there are things more powerful than she, that there are things that can make her cry, that there is a limit to her invincibility.*

I was a little bit drunk. But she smiled at my red face and glittering eyes, talked about my deceased singer, whom she knew and on whom, it turned out, she had had a crush as a young girl.

'No, you just can't imagine, Sonechka, how splendid he could be when he put on his lemon–yellow trousers in the second act of *Onegin* . . . But his voice began to go early on. He drank like a Swede.'

'Before his death they sent him some semolina from the Petrocommune,' I said.

After dinner they got ready to go out, and I started saying goodbye. But before letting me go, Maria Nikolaevna detained me in the living room.

'Until tomorrow,' she said. 'It's good, very good, working with you. I think you have a real gift for accompanying. That happens so seldom. You played Schubert – but don't do that any more, that's not for you. You and I will be marvellous together, though, I can tell. And you? Do you like it with me?'

I barely managed to mumble a few words.

'Well, goodbye. I have to go and dress. Sonechka, would you mind dropping a letter in the post for me? Not the box here on the corner – they haven't picked up from there for a year – but on Liteiny, on the left.'

'Yes, Maria Nikolaevna.'

At that point I noticed that we were alone, that Pavel Fyodorovich was not in the room.

She gave me a stiff blue envelope and I left. On the staircase it was dark, and I made my way to the ground floor by touch, nearly slipping on the icy steps. On the street there was also utter darkness, and the snow sparkled of its own accord – there were neither streetlamps nor a moon. Just stars. I walked as far as Liteiny. I couldn't read to whom the letter was addressed. Nowhere along the street, neither to the left nor to the right, was there a single light. I couldn't see two feet in front of me, so I followed the walls of the buildings in order not to stumble on a snowdrift or a post. I stopped at the postbox. By the light of the stars I tried to read the address. I got the idea that if I could decipher even just the first letter of the name (it should have started with an S), I wouldn't drop the letter in but take it home, open it, read it, and send it the next morning. I gave it a long hard look, and my eyes filled with tears. Finally I made out a tall skinny A. And all of a sudden I could read it, as if lightning had flashed behind me: 'Andrei Grigorievich Ber, 19 Zverinskaya Street.' I don't know why I got scared. I dropped the letter in the box and stood there for a while, my heart pounding.

Past me walked two men, two tramps, apparently. They were carrying something big and heavy. It seemed like a door. That terrified me even more. Suddenly shots rang out in the direction of the bridge. I started to run. For some reason I tried to recall the face of Pavel Fyodorovich but couldn't. I tried to recall his voice and what he had said. And I couldn't. I wanted to think about whether she loved him and he loved her. Who was he? What did he do? What would come of the three of us after this? And I couldn't. She lingered in my thoughts. Her voice. Her almost overly wilful, self-assured way with people, with the future. And about the fact that she had an indisputable right to that attitude vested in her from above and for all time.

FOUR

———◦❧◦❧———

MORE THAN two months passed. Every day I was at the Travins. I worked with Maria Nikolaevna, ate dinner, once in a while stayed on in the evening to play draughts with Pavel Fyodorovich. But neither 'Senya' nor 'Andrei Grigorievich Ber' did I set my eyes on or hear a word about. At home all went on as it had, but I was gradually breaking away from my old life. Mama, her cares, her indispositions, left me unconcerned. Mitenka was having his first romance with X.'s granddaughter – with whom, according to general opinion, he was in love strictly out of inertia. Mitenka so admired the grandfather, a very famous composer. However, Mitenka had no thought of imitating X.; he was getting deeper and deeper into his chorales and was even planning to build some kind of special piano with four keyboards on which to perform them. But enough of Mitenka. Having set me up with Travina, he gradually dropped out of my life. I met up with him again in Paris, relatively recently. But more of that in due time.

Other acquaintances who might have come to see me, with whom I might have been linked by some kind of feeling, I didn't have. Anyway, everything past now seemed to me worthless memories – all in fact being forgotten. In the morning I practised, stood in line for food, stoked the stove; after lunch, which always consisted of the same thing – herring and *kasha* – I washed the dishes, got washed myself, changed into my one decent dress, and left.

It was warm there. They fed me there, told me that life was a hard but engrossing thing. Sometimes they gave me a present. Maria Nikolaevna, who early in the day was somewhat scattered and charmingly quiet, by seven o'clock got livelier, more down-to-earth. Pavel Fyodorovich sometimes returned a little earlier and sat in the corner of the living room listening to us. But more often as soon as he arrived we sat down to the table. Within a week I already knew their whole life, and it made me laugh to think that on the first day I had been so worked up, out of curiosity and, God knows, various other emotions. Pavel Fyodorovich worked in one of the state food supply centres, where he could get anything he needed, right down to fresh-killed poultry and museum-quality antiques. He wasn't exactly making a fortune at his job, but he simply did not see any need to be overscrupulous. He liked to live well, lavishly, on a full belly. Just two years before he had become very rich, incredibly rich even, richer than anyone I knew, richer than Mitenka's parents. And now he wanted to live prosper-

ously, if not luxuriously, oblivious to everything. And strange though it may seem, he did just that. The main change in their life consisted in the fact that they both were gradually losing their former circle of friends and were not making any effort to acquire a new one. What's there to say? Some had been executed; others were in prison; most had fled; still others had dropped them because they considered Travin a scoundrel. A few actresses, relatives, former employees of Pavel Fyodorovich came by, but that was scarcely the 'society' in which Maria Nikolaevna had so recently sparkled.

Early in April Maria Nikolaevna proposed that I move in with them. They were getting ready to leave for Moscow, the apartment having been sold to some Oriental consul. This last week in Petersburg passed for me like a single day. I was given dresses, I was given money for the hairdresser. Maria Nikolaevna suddenly invaded my life. There wasn't a thing she didn't ask me about: what time I got up; which side I slept on; what colour looked best on me; was anyone courting me; did I believe in God? In short, I felt that suddenly I was utterly defenceless against her, that before I knew it she would find out absolutely everything about me, including what I felt and thought about her. She had such persistence about everything she did, that it was futile to resist her. One more minute of this – that evening (three days before our departure) – telling her about my background, and I might have burst into tears, I was in such a state. She realized she had taken

her questioning too far. (She actually did ask me whether I loved anyone and I quickly said no, because by then Evgenii Ivanovich was utterly forgotten and during those weeks I had grown very distant from mama, so if I did love anyone at that moment, then only her, Maria Nikolaevna Travina, of course.) She realized she had gone too far and that it was time to put an end to our chat. She stood and said:

'Let's do some singing, shall we?'

She was capable of vast quantities of work; 'condition' and 'mood' were not at issue for her. She was preparing for her Moscow concerts. On the eve of our departure she gave her last performance in Petersburg, and that was the day of my first appearance with her.

Dozens of times after that I walked out with her on stage, but I never did learn how to bow, where to look, whether or not to smile at the applause, or how many paces to walk behind her. I walked across quickly, like a shadow, without looking at the audience, I sat down with my eyes lowered and placed my hands on the keyboard. She, on the other hand, passed out smiles and glances as if she had nothing on her mind other than, 'Here am I. Here are you. Would you like to listen? I'll sing for you right now. What a joy it is to give you pleasure.'

That was how I read her thoughts, it seems to me, that time in Petersburg, when she was already standing in front of me in the round indent of the piano. 'Sonechka!' she whispered, and I realized, first, that I should start and, second, that she was the singer and I

was the accompanist, that this concert was her concert, not 'ours', as she used to say, that the glory was
for her, that the happiness was for her, that someone
had tricked me, cheated me, deceived me, put his
thumb on the scale, that I had been made a fool of by
God and fate.

The immense hall was full. During the interval
young people pushed their way into the dressing
room, where we were surrounded by the entire elite
of the Conservatory and the Mariinsky Theatre. I
stood mutely, and from time to time Maria
Nikolaevna introduced me to people who came up.
The majority of them I knew, but it seemed impolite
for me to talk with them, and anyway I had nothing
to say. Someone praised me and asked me to repeat
my name, but then Pavel Fyodorovich came up and
everyone started laughing at something and talking
all at once.

'Sonechka, my handkerchief is somewhere,' Maria
Nikolaevna whispered to me, a frightened look in her
eyes. 'I think I have a runny nose.'

Responding instantly, I started searching for the
handkerchief, found it under a chair, and handed it to
her.

Mama was right there. She had a happy face and a
nose slightly reddened from emotion. She was able to
whisper to me:

'Your first triumph, Sonechka!'

I looked at her in amazement – no, she wasn't
laughing at me.

Because it was April and the clock had been set ahead three hours, the night was perfectly bright; we got home after midnight. I heard Pavel Fyodorovich eat supper alone in the dining room standing at the sideboard; I heard Maria Nikolaevna calling someone on the telephone. At night one could make connections only with difficulty. For a long time she couldn't get through. Then she was talking – very quietly, very quietly. I didn't move. I could have put my ear to the door and picked up every word, but I didn't budge. I sat on the bed. What business was it of mine that she had a lover, or two? Let Pavel Fyodorovich kill her or them, or let her lay hands on herself. What about me? What was I going to do with my life? What about me? Why was I put on this earth?

Suddenly the door opened and she walked in:

'You're not asleep yet? Let me give you a kiss. Thank you for this evening.'

I took her hand and mumbled: 'What are you saying, Maria Nikolaevna? What did I have to do with it?'

She poked a prune in my mouth and laughed.

The next day at eight in the evening we left for Moscow.

Mama was at the station, as was Mitenka, and X.'s granddaughter, and another thirty-odd people whom I knew slightly or not at all. Maria Nikolaevna was standing at the window of the sleeping car wearing a white kidskin cap and a white fox over her shoulder. I was trying to figure out which of the men she looked

at most often, but mama, all teary-eyed, at an utter
loss for words, went and got in between her and me.

'Come back, my little girl,' she said. 'What's going
to become of us all? My shining light, be happy! God
grant the Travins health, they've been so good and
kind. Be careful, watch out, work hard . . . Sonechka, my little one . . .'

I listened to her babbling, and although I couldn't
make out half of it, some of those last words reached
me in those minutes. 'Mamochka,' I told her, 'everything's going to be fine, mamochka. See how well
everything's going as is? What's there to worry about?
You don't need to worry. Stay well, mamochka.' She
was crying and kissing me. The bell rang. I hopped up
onto the steps. At that moment out of the crowd
seeing us off stepped a man in a military jacket with
chevrons and a shiny holster at his belt. He took two
steps towards the car, firmly shook Pavel Fyodorovich's dangling hand, kissed Maria Nikolaevna's
hand two times, and waved his cap. Everyone was
waving hats and scarves, even Mitenka. The man in
the military jacket, taking big steps, stayed next to
the window.

'We'll see each other in Moscow,' he said.

'Enough, you're going to fall under the train,' she
replied.

'We'll see each other in Moscow,' the man repeated, as if it were a threat.

The train started to pick up speed and he was left
behind.

'Senya has grown so fat,' said Pavel Fyodorovich, addressing me, 'that before he knows it he won't be able to run any more.'

Maria Nikolaevna said nothing. She was standing at the window looking back. From the direction of her gaze I could tell that she was looking not towards the people seeing us off, in the forefront of whom Senya was waving his cap, but off to the left, sadly, lingering.

We had two adjoining compartments. Travelling with us in the car were some high Soviet officials, with whom Pavel Fyodorovich, who had business in Moscow, immediately became acquainted. First they drank in our compartment, and then we drank in theirs. Maria Nikolaevna, wrapping herself in a large, brightly coloured shawl, kept one of them on his knees in front of her for about half an hour holding a full goblet of wine in his hand. Pavel Fyodorovich was having a long, animated conversation with another about hunting, Karakhan's famous gun collection, and the Tsar's aurochs hunts. The third, a skinny young man with an angelic face and big eyes, demanded categorically that he and I drink to the familiar 'thou'. I was scared, but I let him take my hands and held out my glass, after which he said he was going to kiss me. I got even more scared. I realized that I had drunk too much and could fall in love with him if he did that.

'I'll teach you how to kiss,' he said. 'It doesn't matter that you don't know how, I'll teach you.'

From the opposite corner of the compartment Maria Nikolaevna said:

'Easier said than done.'

He kissed me, and I felt something tender and moist in my mouth.

The night was flying through the window, someone was staggering through the corridor, someone was kissing my hands, not importunately, very cautiously; finally someone gently led me back to my compartment. The night was flying through the window. The train was speeding. I felt life flying towards me, and I speeding towards it, into velvety darkness.

FIVE

SENYA ARRIVED in Moscow two weeks after we did. I waited for him the way people must wait for someone they love. Meanwhile, time was racing on, precipitously, decisively, and each day of Moscow life brought something new.

We were staying with Maria Nikolaevna's sister, on the Spiridonovka. The first floor of the house was taken up by some governmental office; the second housed fifteen people, all related. Only I was an outsider.

From the first day of our arrival various loutish gentlemen came to see us; they did not ask when and where Maria Nikolaevna was going to sing or what she was going to sing. Rather they commandeered her, gave her orders, politely it's true, but brooking no objections: go to a reception in a cart that would be waiting for her at her doorstep; go and sing at the Philharmonic – and at such and such a time and with such and such a programme; accept an engagement at the Bolshoi for the coming winter. Pavel Fyodor-

ovich, who almost never left the house (his business deal proved fictitious), once said:

'We should clear out of here now, not in the autumn. Can you really go on like this?'

Maria Nikolaevna looked at him trustingly, and we all understood that he would start working on false documents the next day.

But apart from this commandeering, I learned something else in Moscow: I learned another's fame to the full extent, and I even got a little used to it. Maria Nikolaevna did not let me leave her side. Once in a while she sent me off to talk with demanding admirers, once in a while she asked me to go somewhere on an errand. I remember at some dinner, after the second concert, I think, she was supposed to sit next to Lunacharsky and at the last moment seated me in her place. Lunacharsky reddened and didn't say a word, but towards the end of dinner he let himself get fantastically presumptuous:

'Are you a virgin or not?' he asked, breathing wine at me. 'Answer me, are you a virgin or not?'

Stammering, I admitted frankly that I was. He announced this to the entire table, shed a tear, and was about to bow at my feet when Pavel Fyodorovich stepped in.

Another's fame, another's beauty, another's happiness were all around me, and the hardest part for me was knowing that they were deserved, that if I were not at the piano on the stage, if I were somewhere where no one noticed me, not somewhere behind

Maria Nikolaevna in the dressing room but in the crowd clapping or running out after her into the passageway, I would have looked at Travina just as ecstatically, would have had the same longing to speak with her, touch her hand, catch a glimpse of her smile. But right now I dreamed of only one thing – finding that strong woman's weak spot, finding a chink for when remaining her shadow became unbearable –and then dealing with her life.

Her relationship with Pavel Fyodorovich surprised me many times. Despite the fact that she undoubtedly had some secret, their relations were unmarred. He loved her as much as anyone can love. They had been married six years. For him, her every word, her every thought was above scrutiny, she was his whole life. And she reciprocated in full. But I was waiting for Senya, to catch her out in her deceit. And one morning Senya did come to see us, straight from the train.

'Take off your cap. What kind of boorish habit is that, walking into a room with your cap on?' she said as she towelled her freshly washed hair. 'Well, what's going on in Petersburg?'

I left the room and stopped outside the door. But their conversation got very quiet very quickly. Senya's spurs clicked twice. When Pavel Fyodorovich came home, I told him, barely concealing my agitation, that someone was with Maria Nikolaevna.

He peeked through the crack of the door and closed it again.

'Someone in riding breeches,' he told me. 'It's probably Senya. So he did come, the ass! Well, let them talk it out.'

We sat for a while in the nursery, which was empty. Half an hour passed. Pavel Fyodorovich showed me some papers and asked me to remember the new names we would be using when we set out for the south the following week. I was awfully nervous, and it was strange to me that he was absolutely calm. All of a sudden they came out into the foyer. We could hear two people coming out, but neither Maria Nikolaevna nor her guest uttered a single word. Senya slammed the front door.

'He's still clinging to those crazy hopes,' said Maria Nikolaevna, coming in to where we were. 'It's all so hard. Fifteen years of genuine friendship. A light-hearted, intelligent man, and I've lost him.'

And she sat down.

Pavel Fyodorovich asked:

'You weren't cruel, I hope?'

'Rather,' she replied, and leaning forward on her arm, she became pensive.

I was standing by the window, my arms hanging straight at my sides. I wanted to throw myself at them both and ask them to drive me away.

'Well, I have some news, some capital news,' Pavel Fyodorovich began to say. 'Everything's set, and I think we can be moving shortly.'

Maria Nikolaevna raised her head.

'Hateful Moscow,' she said. 'North, south, I don't

care which direction, just so long as we get away.'

And five days later we did.

Our journey was secret and dangerous. It cost a lot of money and valuables and took about a month. But despite all its exceptional moments it was too much like other similar journeys, and if during our wanderings it seemed that only we were fated to pick lice off ourselves, to be robbed down to our last kopek, to hide in a freight car that had survived the dynamited railways, then upon our arrival in Rostov we found out that dozens, hundreds of people had lived the same experience, and amid the general gaiety and plenty no one gave it another thought. Now we had an apartment in a hotel. Pavel Fyodorovich within a few days had closed some deal for nearly a million, Maria Nikolaevna was rehearsing, performing, shining. As for me . . . I was in love for the first time in my life. We would go to Filippov's to eat pastries. He was eighteen, in his first year of university, and his innocence moved me to tears.

We went through everything: 'If I go away to war, will you cry?'; and 'I've lived through too much in life not to realize . . .'; and 'If you can't obey me totally, then say so.' Infinitely sweet and utterly empty words that hurtled me into blissful paralysis.

At home I concealed my friendship. I was trying to be my usual competent and docile self. Every day Maria Nikolaevna rehearsed; there were performances, primarily for charity; and here once again was the same success that enveloped her everywhere, like air.

And I thought of how my college boy and I would get married and I would leave the Travins – without giving notice, without saying goodbye – and start my own life, have a child, and abandon music, which had played such a cruel joke on me. And in these thoughts I was almost happy.

'Sonechka, sit down here beside me,' Maria Nikolaevna said to me one day. 'After all, you're my friend, so I can speak openly with you, can't I?'

'Yes, Maria Nikolaevna.' I sat down where she indicated.

'Look at me. Lately your eyes have changed: they've grown very hard. Give up your boy. He's very silly.'

I turned cold.

'All right, if he were only young, or innocent, or ugly, or something else. But yours is simply silly. God only knows, but it's impossible to look at him without laughing.'

'How did you find out?'

'There's nothing to find out even. Don't tell me it's the real thing?'

'We're getting married,' I squeezed out.

'It can't be! No, this has got to be a joke. Don't you know he's going to end up a telegraph operator?'

'Why a telegraph operator? He's in law school.'

'That doesn't matter, he's still going to be a telegraph operator. And he's going to have toothaches all his life.'

(Indeed, he had had an abscess recently.)

' . . . and when you go walking with him arm in arm –'

'Maria Nikolaevna, stop it!'

'Why should I? This is life. God's world is arranged marvellously, isn't it?'

I was sitting in silence. It would have been better if she'd said: I forbid you to get involved with that simpleton, or something of the sort. Yes, in comparison with her, all people were pitiful and silly.

'And then, you know, we'll be going soon.'

'Where?'

She walked up to me, put her hand on my shoulder, and looked – not at me, at her hand.

'A-broad,' she said, barely audibly, as if the walls had ears.

So I didn't see my college boy again. Suddenly I realized that my romance with him was a digression from the main plot line I had picked up back in Petersburg. I realized that there could be no one else in my life but the Travins. And once again I started scrutinizing everything, paying closer attention to them, but I never came up with anything that was of any use to me.

We truly did leave Rostov in the autumn, arriving in Constantinople via Novorossisk. Pavel Fyodorovich made our life easy and carefree – this second journey was safer and simpler than the first, but my nomadic existence would come to an end only in the spring of 1920, lasting exactly a year, and I never got what I'd hoped for out of it. I became accustomed to the Travins, I became a member of the family, I was Maria Nikolaevna's principal audience and at the same time

– her servant. And behind both her and Pavel Fyodorovich there was gradually and decisively dispersing
the smoke of some trouble and secret which had
worried me for a long time, but I knew that the day
would come when it would once again coalesce and I
would find out everything I wanted to know.

So, in the spring of 1920, our third journey came to
an end: we were in Paris.

I remember, it was raining, it was evening, I was
looking out of the window of the taxi at the street, at
the passers-by – I was sitting in the forward seat,
opposite the Travins. Maria Nikolaevna looked tired. I
remember my dreams in my room at the Hotel Regina,
those first days, the photo of Maria Nikolaevna in the
Petit Parisien. I remember all of it precisely, as if it
were yesterday. Life once again, for the umpteenth
time that year, was starting all over again, tempestu-
ous, colourful, and generous. The Travins' old friends
turned up, there were evenings out, parties,
restaurants. Summer came and Maria Nikolaevna left
for the mountains; Pavel Fyodorovich left soon after.
I lounged around town, saw Napoleon's tomb,
churches; I had money aplenty. Later they sent for me
from the south. We returned in September and work
went right into full swing: Pavel Fyodorovich immer-
sed himself in business, Maria Nikolaevna began
preparing for her concerts. An impresario came on the
scene – a shark and a scoundrel, but a charming man
full of jokes, compliments, and every possible service.
It was autumn.

The day it happened I was alone at home. We already had our own apartment. The Travins had gone out for lunch somewhere, and the maid had the day off.

Someone rang at the door.

I was working something out on the piano and without giving a single thought to who it might be I went to open it.

A tall, very tall, still young man walked in wearing a soft hat and coat which, although quite fine, was already well worn. In his hands he carried an old, unfashionable cane.

The door to the living room was open. I saw that he had dark brown hair, that he had a long, straight nose and a small moustache. His eyes looked around unhappily.

'Does Maria Nikolaevna live here?' he asked.

'Yes.'

'Is she at home?'

'No, she's not.'

He sighed with relief.

'Might she perhaps return soon?'

I guessed that he had taken me for the maid.

'I don't think so.'

'And Pavel Fyodorovich?'

'He went out as well.'

'Will they be coming back together?'

'I think so, yes.'

He paused. Then he took a slip of paper and a pencil out of his pocket and wrote something.

'Here is my telephone number,' he said. 'Take it. Give it to her.' He stressed 'her'. 'Tell her that Ber came, Andrei Grigorievich Ber. You won't forget?'

And he slipped two francs into my hand.

I took the money, thanked him, and said with complete conviction: 'No, I won't forget. Don't worry.'

When he left, I sat down on a velvet stool right there in the foyer and began to cry.

SIX

I KNEW I was going to have to tell Maria Nikolaevna that Ber had come, the very same Ber whom I had forgotten all about in the intervening months, indeed had only sensed, the way a dog does, his existence in the world. The very same man to whom, that first evening of my employment with Maria Nikolaevna, I had dropped the letter in the postbox on Liteiny. Now he was in Paris. Was he following our trail? I was prepared to vouch that that was not so. Undoubtedly he had left Russia via the north and here he was, and this was his first (after a year's absence) appearance in Maria Nikolaevna's life.

Isn't that enough for you? I told myself. *Are you so badly off? What are you after, and why are you looking to destroy this life when they've accepted you so trustingly?* I grabbed the narrow pier glass with both hands and looked into it, at my face, as if I had never seen it so close up. And the more I looked, the more it seemed to me that it wasn't I doing the looking but someone looking out at me from the mirror. That she had the eyes of a person who had decided to set fire to the ancestral home. That her large, pale, veiny hand perhaps already clutched a smoking fuse.

'A fuse? What fuse is that?' And in the mirror behind me I saw a laughing face. Maria Nikolaevna had entered the room without a sound. 'Pavel Fyodorovich went to the races, and I came back. Please, would you mind plugging in the iron? I have something to be pressed for this evening. Where's Dora?'

Dora was the maid.

'I'll press it, Maria Nikolaevna. Dora's out.'

We were standing in the middle of the room. When I saw that she was standing directly opposite the light, so that her face could not hide a single movement from me, I unclenched my fist and gave her Ber's telephone number.

'A gentleman came to see you and asked that you call him.'

She said 'ooph' and sat down.

'What does he want? Who is he? Maybe he was looking for Pavel Fyodorovich?'

'No, he wanted you. Andrei Grigorievich Ber.'

Well, now are you satisfied? She's turned white. Enough. Enough. The rest has nothing to do with you. She's gone utterly pale, she's going to be sick. Are you happy now? See how badly she's taking it . . .

But Maria Nikolaevna did not feel at all poorly, and she was merely shaking her head, not tottering as I had imagined. She took the piece of paper, read it, thought. I stood and waited.

'The iron,' she said, not looking at me. 'Sonechka, I asked you . . .'

I went to the kitchen and put the iron on. It was quiet in the rooms.

'While it's heating,' she called out suddenly in her strong voice, 'Sonechka! Please! Call this number!'

We went to the telephone.

'Ask for Mr Ber and say that you told me he was here but I'm so busy these days, so busy, that I beg him to forgive me – I can't see him. I'll let him know when I'm freer.'

Her cheeks were flaming, her eyes gleamed, her voice was on the verge of cracking.

I called and was told that Ber was not at home. That was one thing she hadn't expected. She became distraught and started fiddling with her heavy bracelet, taking it off and putting it on again. I went back to the kitchen.

Half an hour later she called me in. She wanted to sing a little before dinner.

'What do you think, Sonechka,' she said when she was already standing at the piano and looking at me strangely. 'If I were to try to find out someone's address from their telephone number, would that be possible?'

'I think so.'

'No, not Ber's! Oh, you're so sly, you were probably thinking about that Ber. I'm just asking theoretically.'

'Yes, I think there's a special telephone book. When we were staying at the Regina I saw it.'

'A special one? What if I don't have it?'

'Then you'll have to go through the entire telephone book – a million numbers.'

'A million, great! Just how many hours do you think that would take?'

How should I know? I was preoccupied with one thought: Would she ask me not to say anything about Ber's coming in Pavel Fyodorovich's presence or not? But Pavel Fyodorovich came back (with hefty winnings and as cheerful as ever), and Maria Nikolaevna had said nothing to me.

She didn't say anything to him either, though.

'No one came?' he asked while he was still in the foyer.

And I answered, 'No one, Pavel Fyodorovich,' expecting a grateful look in return, but Maria Nikolaevna didn't even turn her head in my direction.

The following morning, at her request, I got through to Ber and relayed her message. She listened in on the receiver. He asked me to repeat the message and thanked me. The evening of that same day Maria Nikolaevna talked Pavel Fyodorovich into taking her to a certain gambling house where, unlike most clubs, they let in women (secretly, of course). They got back late. Maria Nikolaevna woke me up coming into my room.

'On an occasion like this,' she said, sitting down on my bed, 'it's all right even to wake up this sleepyhead Sonya. I lost eighteen thousand, and Pavel Fyodorovich not only didn't yell at me, he tried to console me. (And they call him a "merchant"!) Then I got it back and took away still another seven thousand. It takes skill to gamble! It's not like singing! Anyone can sing!'

She was so pretty, so thrilled, that Pavel Fyodorovich and I didn't know how to calm her. All three of us fell asleep just before dawn. *'They call him a "merchant".'* *Who calls him a merchant?* I thought. *Who has the right to tell her that Travin is a merchant?* But there was something about Pavel Fyodorovich, I understood that, that might grate on people outside his circle.

In the past year he had completely changed his appearance. He had rid himself of his 'merchant' haircut and now combed his hair with a parting, European fashion. Instead of tall boots he wore the best quality shoes, and in winter pale grey gaiters. His linen, ties, suits – everything he had was exquisite. His hands were well groomed, his face rounded out, and he wore a diamond ring on his hairy little ring finger. And when he was neither talking nor moving about, but smoking a cigar in an armchair, his legs outstretched, his already considerable stomach presenting in front, one might take him for a wholly respectable person, for a gentleman, on the verge of venerability.

But all he had to do was start talking or walking about to reveal quite suddenly a certain merry vulgarity, a certain animalness, a primitiveness. It was obvious that more than anything in the world he preferred to eat and drink well, to have a snooze, to take a flyer, as he put it, to show off Maria Nikolaevna – all of which rather shocked some of his acquaintances but which didn't bother Travina herself in the slightest. She said she thought that a man should be exactly like that: crude in his tastes, stable in life, indifferent to whether or not he was making a suitable impression on people who meant nothing to him. That was almost exactly what she once told me:

'There's something untenable, unnatural, in two people: when he is preoccupied with his thoughts, goes off on a tangent of his own, sees nothing around him, steps in every puddle, misses the chair when he sits down, blows his nose in his napkin; whereas she is always calculating how much everything costs, and whether or not his galoshes are leaking, and oh! tomorrow the rent is due, and something else as well. A man has to be sober-minded. If he has to, push his neighbour out of the way so that he himself can pass. A woman – perhaps you think she should be some kind of bird? No, not at all. But if she has some talent, or at least a heart, she is saved.'

That is what she once told me. And that evening when she went out alone – something she had never done before – I recalled those words of hers and thought that it's just as easy to deceive the man who lives in his own world, who makes a fool of himself, who acts like an utter dolt, and the man who is a sober, solid being, who loves life and is loved by life in return.

She went out in the evening. Pavel Fyodorovich was at the club. She didn't say where she was going. She came back shortly after, at about eleven, she couldn't have gone far; maybe she went for a ride in the Bois de

Boulogne, maybe, like a little 'midinette', she sat for a while in a corner café. She went into her room. Usually I was not asleep at that time, but that evening I wasn't feeling well and had taken to my bed. When I heard her in her room I threw on a robe and slippers and ran to ask whether she wanted tea in bed. I knocked on her door and, since no one answered, quietly walked in. Maria Nikolaevna was sitting on the chair by her dressing table crying.

I ran to her wildly, not understanding what I was doing and feeling like I was crying as well. I grabbed her hand and with my other arm embraced her and splattered her dress with tears. She covered her face with her hand. My chest was heaving. I couldn't get a word out. Finally she gently pushed my head back and looked me in the eyes. I had the feeling she was just about to tell me . . . that she couldn't hide it any longer. Oh, how, how I wanted that! But she simply smiled at me.

'Let's have some tea,' she said. 'All this will pass.' And she dusted my still wet eyes and hers with a big pink powder puff.

An hour later I was in my room, alone. So there, she had cried. Enough. The very thing I had dreamed of had happened without me. She had cried, suffered; she had not been happy.

But the next day – which was for some reason especially frantic and overbusy – in looking at her, so even, so calm, so unclouded, I scarcely believed myself. The further that evening receded, the more I began to wonder – had I really seen her tears? Was it possible there had not been any at all, and that it was only weariness? Or maybe she had cried for completely different reasons having nothing to do with Ber or with Pavel Fyodorovich. Maybe she had lost her favourite bracelet or received bad news from her relatives in Moscow?

A week later she sang at the Gaveau Concert Hall.

A low-cut sky-blue evening dress was made for me, the hairdresser did my straggly, dry hair, trying to give it life and shine. Maria Nikolaevna was unusually pretty in her white dress with her black braid wound around her head. Her dress, in the current postwar fashion, did not button but was somehow wound and secured, and that amused her greatly. 'What would happen,' she told Pavel Fyodorovich when we were riding in the taxi, 'if your trousers wrapped around you like an envelope? What would you say?'

In a dusty room backstage we were met by people with flowers; the impresario, whose beard that day was dyed almost navy, gasped when he saw Maria Nikolaevna. Then he saw me.

'How – young – you are!' he wheezed ecstatically. Yes, I was young. There wasn't much more to say about me.

And so we walked out. She ahead and I behind, past the first row of people sitting on the stage who, like those in the hall, of course, looked right past me at her. I always accompanied her from memory. I had the idea that if I accompanied her from the music, that someone else would have been walking behind me, say, another young girl, but in a pink dress, and she would have sat beside me on the bench and turned pages for me. That is, she would have been to me approximately what I was to Maria Nikolaevna. But I played from memory, and there were only two of us. There were two of us on stage, and I had the impression that there were two of us in the hall. I knew that Pavel Fyodorovich had gone to the first box from the right, where some acquaintances were sitting. The hall was packed. But I still felt as if there were only the two of us. That sensation continued, probably, for a minute: from the moment the applause ceased until I suddenly caught sight of Ber in the first row.

He was looking at her, he was as pale as the white front of his evening clothes. There were now three of us. I played the first chord. Maria Nikolaevna looked over the audience. But I guessed that she knew he was there. Even if she didn't look at him, she still saw him.

SEVEN

WINTER CAME. After the first concert there were still two more, and by December Maria Nikolaevna had two engagements: one for America, a concert tour; the other to Milan, at La Scala. She was now so closely and thoroughly surrounded by people that the two of us were alone only in the morning, before lunch, when she practised, sometimes before dressing; she was alone with Pavel Fyodorovich only late at night, when they got back from wherever she had been – visiting, the theatre, a nightclub. The three of us were never together the way we had been at all any more.

An incredible number of old acquaintances turned up: wheeler-dealers of the same ilk as Pavel Fyodorovich; actress friends; society ladies; ageing young people; even foreigners.

There was always someone there for lunch, and by midday – if the Travins were eating in – sometimes five or six people had come by. Some of them were there day in and day out; others varied. Sometimes I didn't even know who they were or what to call them.

Muscovites surfaced (Pavel Fyodorovich was a Muscovite); that year they had converged on Paris, and the Travins' house was high on their list.

Some evenings there was a big card game in Pavel Fyodorovich's study, until eight or so in the morning, so that I was awakened by loud and hoarse parting exclamations in the foyer, when the tobacco smoke finally penetrated as far as my room, having spread throughout the Travin apartment. Pavel Fyodorovich went quietly into the bath and then stretched out somewhere on a couch, slept until one, had breakfast, and drove to the office – to buy and sell Russian timber, oil, coal, gold – in short, everything that had ceased to exist but that he wished still did as before, when he worked in the state food supply centre, in Petersburg, and there administered consignments of paraffin, matches, and salt, of which there were always precisely enough to divide up between himself and a few of his subordinates. And again he gave utterly no thought to whether this was honest or dishonest, whether it would come out equitably or inequitably. Life streamed by, fast and turbulent, and in that turbulent water he sailed.

Every day new people came to our house – young, old, rich or already having squandered their wealth on some speculation; women, for the most part beautiful; men who – whether sincerely or not – treated 'la Travina' like a goddess. But in that flow I never saw the one who, it seemed, it would have been so easy for Maria Nikolaevna to bring into her home; I never saw

Andrei Grigorievich Ber. And because of that I understood that Pavel Fyodorovich knew all about Ber and
that he couldn't come to the Travins' house here, just
as he couldn't in Petersburg.

It became clear to me that Andrei Grigorievich had
played an important part in Maria Nikolaevna's life
before this and that that part was at one time so
obvious to Pavel Fyodorovich that now Ber was barred
entry to the Travins' home – otherwise, had they not
known each other or had Pavel Fyodorovich not
suspected anything, then Andrei Grigorievich could
have paid his visits just like all the other men.
Gradually it became clear to me that Ber had become
Maria Nikolaevna's secret back in Petersburg and now
she was not revealing his presence in Paris to Travin.
She was very quiet. She was often very quiet. She
seemed to take pleasure in the fact that around her
others were talking, making noise, laughing, so that
she hardly had to say anything at all.

Ber's telephone calls and his visit were a thing of the
past. Maria Nikolaevna's life was filled with singing,
entertainments, feminine attentions to her appearance. Seemingly she had neither the opportunity nor
the time to see him, but nonetheless I had no doubt
that she did. Why? I had no proof whatsoever. At the
first concert he sat in the pit and did not come
backstage; I didn't see him at the second or third. Once
Maria Nikolaevna received a letter by mail which she
herself immediately burned in the fireplace, which
was never lit (in all likelihood the flue was shut), and

the ashes flew all over the room. In the afternoon she went out almost daily – not for long, but she went no matter what. She became rather reserved; a shadow of disquiet flitted across her face every so often. And now here she was refusing to go to America or Milan.

'Don't you see – Ber is in Paris!' I wanted to shout at Pavel Fyodorovich when I saw the surprise on his face.

'But why, Masha? This is what you've always dreamed of. You give it some thought . . . Don't you want to?'

She shook her head.

Our 'friends', i.e., four gentlemen who had nothing to do with us, sitting right there were flabbergasted.

I went into Pavel Fyodorovich's study and sat there for a long time staring at a book but thinking my own thoughts, about America, Milan. That was the glory she had been striving for in Russia, and now she was refusing it for the sake of love. She wanted to be with, close to, the man she loved, who had followed her to Paris. To be together. Neither I nor my mother had ever been together with anyone. She was refusing fame for the sake of a few brief, secret meetings. With whom? Who was this Ber? Why didn't he come right out and take her away from Pavel Fyodorovich? What were they waiting for?

I had no answer to any of this. For the time being I knew only one thing: I had discovered Maria Nikolaevna's vulnerability, I knew from which flank to deal my blow. For what? For the fact that she was unique and there were thousands like me? For the fact that her made-over dresses, so flattering to her, did not suit me? For the fact that she didn't know what poverty and *shame* were? For the fact that she could love and I didn't even know what that meant?

'Sonechka,' said Pavel Fyodorovich from the living room, where everyone was sitting. 'Bring me my passports from the centre desk drawer.'

'Why?' I called back, as if I'd been woken up.

'They don't believe I'm forty-seven. They say I'm older. I want to prove it.'

They were having some silly conversation, and she was sitting there, and Travin, who suspected nothing.

I walked over to the desk and pulled open the drawer. There, indeed, lay Travin's five passports, in a large envelope: Soviet, forged, Ukrainian, Turkish, and White. And under them lay a revolver. I immediately shut the drawer. I cannot convey the effect this discovery had on me. It was utterly unlike Pavel Fyodorovich to have a revolver.

I took the passports into the living room. It turned out that Travin really was forty-seven years old. Looking at him you could easily take him for older. Maria Nikolaevna smiled quietly.

'Ber is in Paris.' If I were to utter those words, Pavel Fyodorovich, very likely, might kill me with that revolver. During our travels there had been no revolver. Travelling from Constantinople – I myself had packed Pavel Fyodorovich's bags – there had been no revolver. He had bought it in Paris. When? Why?

And in the living room that inane conversation was

still going on. At eleven a friend of Maria Nikolaevna's came with her husband, and they took her out somewhere. Pavel Fyodorovich and three of his guests sat over a silent game of poker, and I was left with the fourth guest, an elderly, bald man named Ivan Lazarevich Nersesov. He smoked; I sat and waited for him to leave. He didn't like to play poker; he played chemin de fer. He liked to fly in airplanes (at the time, a relative rarity), was a widower, and lived in his own private residence, not far from us.

He smoked in silence, with a lazy, Oriental obliviousness to the whole world; his somnolent eyes looked at me, or so it seemed, without seeing me.

'It's very hard,' he said suddenly.

'What's hard?'

'It's very hard,' he repeated. 'Early to bed, early to rise. It's a bad habit – sitting up at night. Drinking. Eating. Not getting any exercise. Lying about.'

'Yes,' I replied.

'Air,' he said again. 'Sun. I used to love it. Now I've forgotten.'

'You ought to smoke a hookah,' I said. 'Have you ever tried it?'

He shut his eyes affirmatively.

'Let's go,' he said when it seemed to me that he was finally dozing off. 'Pavel Fyodorovich, let the young lady go out with me.'

Pavel Fyodorovich was sitting with his back to us and did not turn around.

'For God's-s-s sake, for God's-s-s sake!' – at that

moment he was thinking something out. 'Where? Go? Sonechka? Sonechka, do you really want to?'

I wasn't dressed when Pavel Fyodorovich came into my room and, ignoring the fact that I covered my shoulders from him, said:

'He is a totally proper man. Just don't drink too much, or you'll get sick. He's a totally proper man. And very boring. Dance with him.'

Nersesov led me out to his motor car. His chauffeur woke up. We got in. I was wearing my blue dress.

'You are sweet, very sweet. So homely and so sweet,' he said. 'So little and so ugly.'

And he laughed. So did I.

We went to a restaurant that was fashionable at the time, and a long, elegant, and indigestible supper began immediately. I drank, Nersesov drank. What did he want with me? He probably hadn't given it much thought. Maybe he was good-hearted and had taken pity on me? Or maybe he was trying to kill yet another sleepless night? I didn't know how to put on powder or perfume; the waiters looked at me sympathetically.

'And you were never in love with anyone, Tanechka?' asked Nersesov. I thought over my life, Evgenii Ivanovich, who left and didn't come back, the tender face in the train between Petersburg and Moscow which I never saw again, my student in Rostov whom Maria Nikolaevna laughed at so. And that was all.

'Not Tanechka. Sonechka,' I replied, and I drank some more.

'You have to get married, dear,' he said. 'You should have kids.'

'Not Olechka. Sonechka,' I replied, and I laughed at myself.

Late, right before dawn, he drove me home, kissed my hand, and thanked me 'for a delightful night of nightclubbing'. I couldn't find the bell right off; when the front door opened, I had the feeling there was someone there in the darkness. I started hunting for the light switch. I felt someone standing very close to me, and I got scared. I left the door to the street open. Suddenly someone walked out and closed it from outside. I turned on the light.

Upstairs the guests had already gone their separate ways. Maria Nikolaevna wasn't back yet. Pavel Fyodorovich was sitting alone in the middle of the living room. It was full of smoke; the rug was crumpled.

'Why aren't you asleep?' I asked.

'I don't feel like it,' he answered. 'Well, did you have a good time?'

But I suddenly started sobbing.

'For God's-s-s sake, for God's-s-s sake!' he cried, just as before, when he had been thinking something out over cards. 'Get to bed right now. You need a good night's sleep.'

And he pushed me through the door as if he were afraid I was about to say too much.

EIGHT

PERHAPS IF during those weeks Maria Nikolaevna had changed, body and soul, had suffered – so that everyone could tell, including me – if she had fallen ill or lost her voice – I don't know, maybe then I would have been satisfied. But apart from a certain quietness that came over her, and very rarely a look of disquiet, I didn't notice anything. Once again she was sweet and attentive to Pavel Fyodorovich, once again she practised hard and a lot, now and then was blindingly gorgeous, and went about her life confidently and freely. I felt as if I were fading before her more and more, whereas she was growing as a singer and approaching, both outwardly and inwardly, a certain *focus*, if that's the word, in her existence, a point which, given her intelligence, talent, and beauty, she was capable of drawing out, in all likelihood, for many years to come.

In her equilibrium there was something so thrilling it frightened me, repulsed me. That she was deceiving Pavel Fyodorovich I had no doubt, but even that she did distinctively, and he himself, most likely unconsciously, was her accomplice: he never questioned her about anything and in that way never compelled her to lie, never degraded her – she simply didn't bring it up. That what she and Ber had was not a casual 'affair' – applied to her, that word sounded as awkward as if crutches had suddenly been propped up against her strikingly 'true' and regular body – that she and Ber had a long-standing, difficult, and possibly hopeless love I also had no doubt. And despite the insolubility of those feelings, she continued to radiate a constant happiness. And for that perpetual happiness I dreamed of punishing her.

Letting Pavel Fyodorovich know that Ber was in Paris was the least of it for me. I needed proof that she was seeing him. What I was going to do with that proof later and how I was going to inform Travin I hadn't yet thought. I was waiting, I was watching.

Chance success was not what I had in mind. That would have been too simple: walking outside and running into them. A few times I had the feeling that Maria Nikolaevna herself was going to bring up the subject of Ber with me. I think that that would have been enough for me to abandon forever all thought of any kind of vengeance against her, of settling accounts with her which only God could have paid. Lately she was less and less often affectionate with me the way she had been in our first months of living together. But once in a while it did happen. I was sitting at the piano, she was standing over me and put her hand on my neck right where I have two stiff tendons and between them a depression. She touched my hair.

'Sonechka, do you ever think of your mama? Of Petersburg? Mitenka?'

'Yes, Maria Nikolaevna.'

'Maybe one day we'll have some news from them. That would be fine!'

I said:

'People keep coming from Petersburg. Maybe a letter will.'

She answered keenly:

'What letter! May the Lord keep you! People are escaping over the ice via Finland . . .'

That was how I found out that Ber had escaped to her via Finland.

As I said, Pavel Fyodorovich left for his office at two o'clock. At four o'clock Maria Nikolaevna went out. If she had a guest she would say: 'I'll be right back.' And the guest, or guests, who, however, were never thought of as such, were left to fiddle on the piano, to leaf through newspapers, to play draughts. Either Dora or I served them tea.

I thought it out in advance. I did not flatter myself with the hope that I would find out everything my first time following her. The first time I went out after Maria Nikolaevna and walked down the street, about thirty steps behind her, I couldn't make myself go beyond the corner, for fear of being noticed. Two days later I went again. Our street intersects another, which lets out onto a large, quiet square with a monument. On the near side is a pastry shop; on the far, three cafés next to each other: two on the corners, relatively spacious and well-lit, and in between a darker, dirtier one, so that anyone who wanted to would certainly stop in at one of the corner ones, never at the middle one, where terrible coffee probably cost twenty-five centimes less than at its neighbours.

Maria Nikolaevna walked as far as the square. Thinking she would take a cab, I went around the other side in order to follow her, taking the last car in line, but Maria Nikolaevna bypassed the taxi stand; she went right through the narrow door of the tiny middle café. And I headed back home.

When I ran into the apartment I still retained the shadow of a doubt. I remembered Ber's telephone number. I dialled. No, he was not home, he left an hour ago. And when would he return?

At that moment I heard someone slipping a key into the lock of the front door. I hung up the receiver, and the telephone jingled. I stood behind the door, hidden by the portière. I saw Pavel Fyodorovich walk in. He walked in as if embarrassed to be at home at such an untimely hour.

His first glance was at the coat rack. No guests. He sighed with relief. He walked past me, into the living room, and from there into Maria Nikolaevna's room. I stole after him – I was almost unafraid: if he looked back I could turn it all into a joke. He stood there for rather a long time, as he was, in his hat and coat, and then walked down the hall to the dining room and twice looked at the clock. 'Sonechka!' he shouted.

I called back from my own room.

'No, it's nothing. I forgot something . . . I had to come back.'

The door slammed. He left. With unaccountable alarm I raced to his study, to his drawer. No, the revolver was in its place. What foolishness I could think up! Who besides me could do anything to make him pick up that revolver and shoot it? But my time had not yet come.

If I could have settled the score with her some other way – openly walk out on her, perhaps take Ber away from her, make it so that her voice paled by comparison with my playing, so that next to me she ceased to exist, if only for one single person. But I had nothing. I had to take my revenge crudely.

I remember the following day. In the morning she vocalized, and for lunch there were two Frenchmen. Pavel Fyodorovich kept them busy with conversation, poured them expensive wine. They discussed who had what kind of cellar. Then the men left. The dressmaker came for a fitting. Then . . .

I went out first. I walked as far as the square, crossed it, and entered the half-dark, empty café. To the left and right were little tables, between them was a narrow aisle, at the end of which was a partition. I went beyond that. There it was even darker. I sat down at the first table in the corner, ordered beer, and opened my newspaper. My calculations proved correct. Ten minutes later Andrei Grigorievich Ber, wearing the same hat, carrying the same stick, walked in and sat in the first section, right by the partition. I saw him through the transparent pattern in the frosted glass, a foot away from me. It was quiet, outside it was raining; it was that special Paris season when in early February it is neither day nor evening and time seems to move more slowly and the city becomes sadder.

Maria Nikolaevna sat down next to him and they were served something. She was here. I still could not believe it. He took both her hands, pulled off her gloves, kissed her hands lingeringly.

'Don't cry,' she said suddenly.

There was a long silence.

'My hands are wet from your tears,' she said again.

A large wall clock ticked above me, in my dark corner; a lorry went by. The fat proprietor dozed behind the zinc bar. And that was it.

'I can't,' she said. 'I gave my word to Pavel Fyodorovich. I can't.'

He said:

'The tears are running down your face too, and your coffee is cold and probably salty.'

She stirred her spoon in her glass. There was something unlifelike in the stillness of their large, dark silhouettes.

'Tell me something,' he said. 'Smile at me.'

But obviously her voice and lips were not obeying her.

'I can't leave him,' I heard. 'It would be the same as up and killing him. And I can't deceive him either.'

'Then I'll go kill him,' he said in a whisper.

Again she was silent for a long time.

'I want to come here and look at you. And you come and look at me.'

He looked at her for a long time.

'Wait a minute,' he said suddenly and smiled. 'Do you really think we can go on like this?'

She rested her cheek on her hand like an old peasant woman. The clock was ticking, time was passing, someone walked in, had a drink at the bar, and clinked his money down. He left.

And when the electric light over the bar, over them, over me, suddenly blazed on, Maria Nikolaevna got up and left. A minute later Ber called the proprietor over, paid the bill, and left as well. Two more lamps went on. Outside all was dark.

I walked out in a stupor. There was no one in the world with whom I could have cried. No one in the world . . . Some streets, streetcorners, streetlamps . . . none of it registered. I reached home and rang. Dora opened the door; Maria Nikolaevna was in her room, and Nersesov was sitting in the living room.

I stood in the doorway for a long time and looked at him, and he at me. Perhaps he did have reason to say that he and I shared some kind of friendship. He was the sole person of the Travins' visitors who now knew my name and didn't get it wrong any more; there was the evening when he had taken pity on me.

I sat down opposite him. I thought: what would it be like if he were my husband, or even just a close friend? Or not even him but someone else, just so I wasn't alone, always alone, but to be two of us, together with someone, so that from time to time it would be like . . . I'd shine his shoes in the morning, I'd iron his handkerchiefs, wipe off his wet razor. I would have dinner waiting for him, I would press close to him sometimes to feel his warmth with my body.

A bald old man sat in front of me.

'Where have you been?' he asked.

'Out walking, Ivan Lazarevich,' I replied mechanically.

'You see I stopped by. Now the Dismans will be coming, and Pavel Fyodorovich will be back. We're to have dinner.'

Dora was setting the table in the dining room. Maria Nikolaevna was giving her instructions. I rose, slowly, dragging my feet, went into Pavel Fyodorovich's study, pulled out the desk drawer without turning on the light, and took out the revolver. Stepping softly, I went out into the hallway, went to my room, and hid the revolver under my pillow.

I decided to kill Pavel Fyodorovich that night.

NINE

————— ⋙◦⋘ —————

IN THE evening we had guests, about ten, but that day there were no cards: Maria Nikolaevna sang.

She never refused when she was asked, but that evening, or so it seemed to me, she agreed grudgingly. The guests sat in a corner of the living room where there was a lamp and deep white armchairs. Lyalya Disman had tossed two pillows on the carpet and stretched out on them; someone else was left in full shadow. Pavel Fyodorovich sat on the end; I could see his face. I saw how from time to time, when it was quiet, he got up, brought someone an ashtray or an orange, grabbed the fruit knife from the bowl and served them, ladled out glasses from a large punch bowl in which chunks of pineapple and peach floated like in an aquarium.

I was seated at the piano. She was standing next to me. She was wearing a dark dress, and she was paler than usual. Her voice sounded magnificent as always, perhaps as never before – but if there was someone that evening who could not listen to her, then it was I.

Free her from Pavel Fyodorovich? From the first notes that rang out above me I realized that that was a freak, pointless idea which had come to me in a moment of weakness, from having overheard her conversation with Ber. No, it was I who needed to free myself from her. The time had come to betray her, to force Travin to pass sentence on her, thereby freeing me to live my own life.

Tomorrow, I told myself. Which one of them he killed was all the same to me. But deal with them he would; and all because of me, me, whom no one listened to and no one noticed, me – nameless, luckless me. There he sat, that sober, sensible man, that 'merchant', who would never suffer anyone short-changing or deceiving him. There he was, with his strong grip on life, for whom all our 'may's' and 'shan't's' were laughable, who his entire life had stepped all over other people without a second thought, who had made his own way and now would never yield any of it. Tomorrow he would find out everything.

But how? How to let him know – that would take careful thought.

In recent weeks he had begun to avoid me for some reason. Twice he had gone away somewhere and I had found out about it on the day of his departure, from Dora. Write him a letter? But signing it would be just like saying it, and if I sent it unsigned he wouldn't believe it. The time had passed when people believed anonymous letters. A hundred years ago they had ruined people's lives; then they had ruined people's days. Now they made people laugh. Call him at the office? He would recognize my voice, and the result would be the same conversation, only coarsened, oversimplified. But I had to put the revolver I'd taken back in its place as soon as possible, and for that I had to wait until the next morning.

So went my thinking, or more accurately, not thinking, for only for brief moments did I retain any thoughts, while Maria Nikolaevna's voice pierced my heart and my eyes stared out to where, leaning back, motionless, with a measure of pomposity that had appeared in him only of late, sat Pavel Fyodorovich.

'Enough. I'm tired,' said Maria Nikolaevna.

But no one felt like leaving as yet. A young, ruddy-faced pianist did a lively rendition of two Chopin études. Lyalya Disman, in her rather crude contralto, sang a few romances which Maria Nikolaevna referred to as 'ambiguous'.

I went to my room, cautiously returning the revolver to the study on my way, and then helped Dora clear the table in the dining room. It was twelve o'clock at night. By one the guests had all gone their way.

The following morning I was awakened by a loud conversation: Pavel Fyodorovich was hurrying Dora with the coffee. Pavel Fyodorovich was leaving for London, on business. His suitcase was already in the foyer. For long? Ten days or so. Maria Nikolaevna, having barely pinned up her braids, was there as well. They said goodbye, he shook my hand.

'Take a look at yourself, Sonechka,' said Maria Nikolaevna. 'You're becoming positively transparent. You and I had better make some changes in our way of life or else we'll perish. Yesterday I sang in a smoky room – I'm good for nothing after that! I mustn't drink wine, or polish off all those unhealthy goodies.'

She was dunking a biscuit into her coffee as she sat across from me.

'And I mustn't be so capricious, and there's lots else I mustn't do – grieve, for instance. Sometimes I do, though. Surprised? Sonechka, today I had a bad dream: hair started growing over my whole face: it started from my brow; my eyes, my nose, my cheeks – and so quickly. I was awakened by my own scream.'

She chattered away for a long time; I scarcely responded. Pavel Fyodorovich's departure had thrown me in a spin. Then Lyalya Disman came over – she had forgotten her gloves at the Travins' the day before. She stayed to lunch and told two jokes of which I understood only one, at which Maria Nikolaevna flushed and said:

'Please, be more careful: our Sonechka is still an innocent.'

At two-thirty Maria Nikolaevna sent me to the library, and from there to buy tickets for the ballet. It was raining so hard that my umbrella had soaked through by the time I reached the corner, so I decided to take a taxicab. In less than an hour her errands had been accomplished. When I walked out of the theatre a feeble sun was trying to break through the raw

February air, and a pale rainbow was falling from the sky. I started for the bus stop. Everything I did that day I did sort of automatically. I felt nothing, thought of nothing other than that Pavel Fyodorovich had gone for ten days. What that might mean I didn't as yet know.

I got off the bus by the pastry shop on our square. The rainbow now was streaming somewhere high up, where a springlike azure was already piercing through. I skirted the monument. In front of the café where at that hour Maria Nikolaevna and Ber were sitting, a huge blue puddle glittered.

They were there. Those streets, that pavement, those glass windows had not existed for me only a few days before, and now at the sight of them a headspinning weakness, an inexplicable pain descended on me. It would have been better not to look at all that; I had waited two years, I could wait another ten days. But still I couldn't tear my eyes away. I stood stock-still, hugging the books and umbrella close. The blue puddle was in the shape of an oak leaf. The bare trees were dropping pearls of light into it. Under the trees was a bench so wet that it looked like it had been lacquered. And on that bench sat Pavel Fyodorovich.

I was shocked that he was here when that morning he was supposed to have departed for London, but I was even more shocked that he was sitting not only without any evidence whatsoever of his recent replete pomposity but in what was for him a strange, utterly uncharacteristic pose of deathly weariness. And I realized why I hadn't recognized him right away.

I walked behind the monument and stood there a little while. When I came out from around it, Travin wasn't there any more. He wasn't on the pavement either. He had left with incomprehensible speed, and perhaps, had I been in a different state, I might have doubted ever having run into him at all. But I had seen everything around me so distinctly – the child's stroller being pushed by a Negress in a green headscarf, the colourful newsstand, the rainbow in the sky – that I had no doubt that Pavel Fyodorovich had just been sitting under those trees and looking directly through the glass door with the sign overhead, 'Liqueurs de marques'. So, he had come back, and maybe he was already home. But where was his suitcase? Would Dora feed him if he hadn't already eaten? So, finally, the time had come to tell him everything, to be alone with him, face to face. To bring him back to this square at the very moment when *they* would be parting.

I ran home, sensing the need to hurry, that life was somewhere close at hand, driving me on, that the clouds were just about to form, the dusk to set in, and there, on the square, the streetlamps to be lit, a reminder that once again it was time to say goodbye. I slammed the front door shut: the lift ascended slowly, soundlessly. I had a key. I unlocked the door and saw Travin's hat and coat hanging in the foyer.

I remember running my hand over the sleeve of his coat – it was thoroughly soaked. I walked into the living room. The piano had been left open, and the white lilac from the day before was rusting and drooping. I approached the study doors. It was quiet in there.

'Pavel Fyodorovich,' I said quietly.

No response.

'Pavel Fyodorovich, may I come in?' And I knocked twice.

In that moment I realized clearly that I would not even make it as far as the leather armchair by the desk, that I would tell all, right here in the doorway, and if he spat in my face I would restrain myself and say nothing.

But there was no response from behind the door.

Then I half-opened it.

Pavel Fyodorovich was sitting at his desk. Dusk was beginning to fall in the room. He was sitting, having pulled out the middle desk drawer, bending over it and examining something in it closely. His left hand dangled between the armchair and the desk; his right lay before him.

'Pavel Fyodorovich!' I cried.

But he didn't stir.

Then I saw that he was dead, that his right hand, dropped on the desk, clutched the revolver.

I started to scream. Dora, separated by three doors, in the kitchen, not having heard the shot, came running at my scream. She lost her head – I don't know what frightened her more: Pavel Fyodorovich's corpse sitting in the study or my long scream, which she couldn't stop and which went on and on. When I try to think of it, it seems to me that it lasted about three days. In fact, Dora had the good sense to splash my face with water, and I quietened down. Ten minutes later she had me settled on the sofa in the living room, where I remained – once again, I don't remember for how long, probably until Maria Nikolaevna's arrival, although right now it seems to me that I lay there a long time, a very long time, even in some way utterly outside time.

That half an hour now seems to me the most unbearable of my entire life, and not only of mine. I think that, all the horror and terror of existence aside, nine out of ten people have never known what I knew then. Between 'it happened' and 'it couldn't *not* have happened' my heart trembled and forsook me. I can neither remember nor explain what I felt then (or thought – it was all the same). About myself, about fate, about people, about happiness, some more about fate, and even about the bullet which only recently had been so close by, which I had aimed into space, and which had, itself, found the spot to which it was destined.

'Be a friend to me, Sonechka,' a voice said above me, a voice I would recognize a thousand years from now, even in utter delirium. 'Help me.'

Maria Nikolaevna raised me from the sofa with both hands. Strangers were standing in the doorway.

TEN

————————◆➣◦➢◆————————

EVERYTHING CHANGED, the life of those two years, the
agitation, the shadowing, everything came to an end,
and all that had happened had happened without me,
apart from me, as if I had never existed in the first
place. I went back to being what I had been at the
beginning, with a feeling of insurmountable weariness in my heart and with a realization of my utter
uselessness. People and passions had passed me by – I
had watched them from my corner, I had rushed at
them so as to ruin something for someone, to help
someone, somehow to assert myself in the process,
and I had been left by the wayside. I had not been
invited to play in the game that had ended in Pavel
Fyodorovich's suicide. He had known all about it
before me. He had understood before me how he
would have to act. He did not try to get even with Ber
and Maria Nikolaevna but stepped aside so that she
could continue living as she pleased and could be
happy with whom she pleased. So that she could be
free.

I grew fond of talking to myself. It was from those monologues of mine, perhaps, that I came to these notes. No one heard me. The nights were moonlit, February nights. I stood in my room at the window without turning on the light, without lowering the shade. The street was silver. I pictured Petersburg, mama, our old, long piano and our two beds alongside it (in the cold months we lived in one room), our two narrow beds covered with white piqué blankets, the small icons tacked up over our beds which in all those years I never did take the time to examine properly. The moon whitened the asphalt, and there was a light frost. I pictured my childhood in N., the creaking gate in the yard, the landlord's dog, which I was afraid of, the cook, who waited with me for mama to come for dinner from her lessons, the poverty, and the sadness, and the orphanhood of our life. The Paris street was quiet and empty; the moon and cold were outside. I pictured life going on right next to me, chafing at people and grinding them down but not including me – no matter how many times I reached out to it.

Pavel Fyodorovich was not on the other side of the wall any more. Maria Nikolaevna was alone, but the people who in recent months had not left her alone with him now too continued to surround her, day and night. They didn't invite her, as before, to go anywhere with them, did not demand expensive wines at dinner, did not talk about the races, the stock market, the tour of the Vienna Symphony. They were simply present: Nersesov and Disman smoked in the living room; Lyalya Disman, sitting Turkish fashion on the bed, tried to embroider something; someone wound the clock that stood in the dining room. In Pavel Fyodorovich's study sat his business partner, a lawyer and former member of the *Duma*, figuring something on an abacus. And this did not surprise Maria Nikolaevna. On the day of the funeral she came back with all of them from the cemetery, and the next day they all gathered together from morning on. I asked her whether the constant presence of people in the house was hard on her. She said that she didn't care, that she would probably be going away soon.

The lawyer, Nersesov, and Disman spoke among themselves about how Pavel Fyodorovich's affairs had taken a sharp turn for the worse of late. Maria Nikolaevna had known that. Yes, Pavel Fyodorovich's affairs in recent weeks had been going downhill, and Maria Nikolaevna could mourn him with a clear conscience, telling herself that not she but money was the cause of his death. Nonetheless, she was well aware of the real cause.

She started to talk to me a week after the funeral. By that time most people had stopped calling on us, and if ever there were outsiders around then it was only for lunch or dinner. One night Maria Nikolaevna came to see me in my room, sat down on the bed.

'You're not asleep, Sonechka?'

'No, Maria Nikolaevna.'

'Is it all right if I sit here a little with you? I love to chitchat with you. Move over a bit.'

I lay there with a pounding heart and looked at her. A light fell on her arms from the adjoining room. She was sitting wrapped in a warm white robe, her thick braid over her shoulders, wearing loose slippers on her rather large, tanned feet.

'What am I to do, Sonechka?' she said softly, clasping her arms and looking at me. 'Here death has grazed me and I still can't shake the feeling of my abiding happiness. Lord knows where it comes from or how it will end . . . Such a great many things have already happened to me, it seems – but still I love life! I don't even know myself how it is I'm breathing, singing, living in this world. Do you blame me?'

'No, Maria Nikolaevna.'

'Others will say that I killed him. But what can I do when I feel no guilt? Do you think he ever blamed me? In that last, the next-to-last, at any moment? No, I know he didn't, and God knows it, too. Where do I get this awareness of my innocence? Is it possible that everyone has it, only others out of hypocrisy hide it?'

I wanted to answer her. I thought for a long time and said:

'There are people like that. There's a kind of magnificence to them. Being with them can be a little terrifying (that's all right, Maria Nikolaevna, don't take this too much to heart). It's rare that anything ever changes or cripples them (that's if we assume that all the rest of us are cripples). I don't know how to say it: happy people, somehow, live above everyone else (and, naturally, rather overwhelm the others). And there's nothing to forgive them for. For them it's like health, or beauty.'

She thought about that and replied, smiling:

'Still, Sonechka, forgive me.'

And we both fell silent. Oh, how unattainable she became for me again with that smile!

And so came the day of our parting. It was summer, the windows were wide open, the apartment had been let, the furniture had been moved into storage. Maria Nikolaevna was going to America with Ber, having signed a two-year contract.

There was nothing left to recall life with Pavel Fyodorovich. Maria Nikolaevna gradually dropped all their former acquaintances, abandoned Pavel Fyodor-ovich's affairs to the mercy of fate, gave up receptions, excursions, financial calculations. She now depended solely on herself, and that independence made her even stronger and younger; in her there appeared the charm one finds in independent women at whom 'society' has thrown up its hands and who have responded to 'society' with total indifference. Recently she had worked a great deal with both me and Ber. I now knew that man quite well. He had ceased to be a riddle to me.

He lived wholly in the future, and not because any kind of 'career' lay before him, or because he had been bestowed with any kind of talent. He had just turned thirty at the time. He was a taciturn man, high-strung, who immediately caught the drift of even a chance companion and easily guessed the thoughts of anyone he knew well. That almost supernatural sensitivity substituted for all other qualities for him: for musicality in music; for a practical grasp in life. He had never shown any particular 'promise', but to look at him, to think about him, it seemed (and not only to me) that the destiny that lay before him might perhaps be somewhat out of the ordinary.

Now he was gradually becoming Maria Nikolaevna's accompanist and manager at the same time. And in a short time he was to become her husband as well. As happens only very rarely, this love had a profound rightness about it in which there was no place for either their jealousy or our doubts. Maria Nikolaevna loved him. Although sometimes it seemed to me that she could have been happy even without love; truly, she needed no one. But him she loved.

They went away, and I – I moved to a hotel. I looked for work. Maria Nikolaevna had given me her promise not to forget me; she left me some money and made a few inquiries for me. And embracing me firmly, she said that if I wanted to go back, to Petersburg, she would arrange that as well.

No, I didn't want to go back to mama.

So she left, and looking at her in those final minutes it seemed to me that she was going not to down-to-earth and, generally speaking, workaday America for work, glory, and a livelihood but to some not entirely real and, of course, happy land forbidden to others and where she was long awaited, already loved, as she herself loved everyone.

Ber, who had once taken me for a servant and tipped me two francs, took little notice of me and was at parting cold with me. I also felt a certain hostility towards him. There wasn't room for both of us alongside Maria Nikolaevna, and I made way for him because I had no other choice. Maria Nikolaevna looked at me long and hard. Perhaps, in saying goodbye to me, she for the first time gave some thought to me, to my life, to my love for her.

I was left on the platform numb, sapped by the receding past, without a present, with a bleak, dark future. I went home to an empty apartment, took my (still Russian) trunk, a bundle of books and music, and asked the doorman to find me a hackney cab. At that time cabs were cheap in Paris: I had suddenly become anxious and parsimonious – I had packed all I owned neatly in the trunk. They placed it at my feet, and I set the books on the seat beside me. I rode through the city and thought that this couldn't be the same Paris but another one, that I was dreaming, that it couldn't be that I was alone in the world, alone, without anyone, without a dream, without whatever it takes to live among you, people, animals, things.

Three years have passed now since I had those thoughts, and in that time I have many times wanted to burrow into the earth like a mole so as not to see or hear anything, or else to cry out that things were not right, were not properly arranged in this world . . . Maria Nikolaevna is still in America.

She is married to Andrei Grigorievich and has no plans to come to Europe. She sings in Philadelphia, goes on tour once or twice a year, and is especially popular in California. She sends me letters, newspaper clippings about herself, sometimes money. I need the money badly: I earn very little – I play the piano in a small cinema on a street leading to Porte Maillot. Our orchestra consists of three people: myself, the violinist who is also the conductor, and the cellist, who also plays the drums and cymbals. Strangely enough, it was Nersesov who found me this job. That was nearly a year after Maria Nikolaevna's departure. Shortly thereafter Nersesov died.

I had already been at that cinema about a year when out of the blue Mitenka arrived from Russia. He sought me out in order to inform me that my mama had died and to give me her (worthless) turquoise earrings. She had been about sixty, it seems. She had caught a chill while out in the countryside looking for food. That hard and strange life, which I had half-forgotten, was still going on there! People lived either like ants or like wolves. In its own way it was a nobler life than ours here.

Mitenka was now married, his wife was pregnant and for some reason hid herself away from everyone. Mitenka was the same as ever – breathed heavily, wheezed, and washed poorly, but he was already well known and had made the transition from *Wunderkind* to outright genius.

'I play in a cinema,' I said, because I had an urge to tell him about myself and not just listen to him.

He inclined his balding head and looked at me sadly.

'Aren't you ashamed,' he said finally, extremely nasally. 'Aren't you ashamed, Sonechka. We had such high hopes for you!'

Dear God, he had mixed me up with someone else – no one had ever had high hopes for me!

Later he invited me to his home, to show me to his wife. She came out, embarrassed, clasping her hands over her belly.

'And this is Sonechka,' he said, 'who I've told you so much about.' Her face registered nothing. 'This is Antonovskaya, Sofia . . .'

He got very upset over having forgotten my patronymic, but I had never had a patronymic, and I made no move to help him out. All that had been a matter of indifference to me for some time.

And truly, is there any point in resenting your own mother for the fact that you had been humiliated before your birth? After all, there were instances – more than one – when just such humiliated individuals turned into wonderful, proud, kind people. The point here lay not in one's birth; the point lay entirely elsewhere. No matter how many times people tell me that a worm could never aspire to world greatness, I'll never stop waiting and telling myself: you can't die, can't let up, not as long as one person is still walking on this earth. There is still one debt which, maybe, one day, you will recover . . . if there is a God.

1936

Nina Berberova was born in Russia and lived there until 1922, when she emigrated first to Berlin and then to Paris, where she lived from 1925 until 1950. At the end of 1950 she moved to the United States, with virtually no money and no knowledge of English. Over the next eight years she held various jobs while studying English at night. In 1958 she became a professor of Russian literature at the graduate school of Yale University, a position she held until 1963 when she moved to Princeton, again as professor of Russian literature in the graduate school. She retired in 1971 and still lives in Princeton, New Jersey.